I'm Going To READ!

These levels are meant only as guides;
you and your child can best choose a book that's right.

Level 1: Kindergarten–Grade 1 . . . Ages 4–6
- word bank to highlight new words
- consistent placement of text to promote readability
- easy words and phrases
- simple sentences build to make simple stories
- art and design help new readers decode text

Level 2: Grade 1 . . . Ages 6–7
- word bank to highlight new words
- rhyming texts introduced
- more difficult words, but vocabulary is still limited
- longer sentences and longer stories
- designed for easy readability

Level 3: Grade 2 . . . Ages 7–8
- richer vocabulary of up to 200 different words
- varied sentence structure
- high-interest stories with longer plots
- designed to promote independent reading

Level 4: Grades 3 and up . . . Ages 8 and up
- richer vocabulary of more than 300 different words
- short chapters, multiple stories, or poems
- more complex plots for the newly independent reader
- emphasis on reading for meaning

LEVEL 2

2 4 6 8 10 9 7 5 3

Published by Sterling Publishing Co., Inc.
387 Park Avenue South, New York, NY 10016
Text © 2006 by Harriet Ziefert Inc.
Illustrations © 2006 by Elliot Kreloff
Distributed in Canada by Sterling Publishing
c/o Canadian Manda Group, 165 Dufferin Street,
Toronto, Ontario, Canada M6K 3H6
Distributed in the United Kingdom by GMC Distribution Services,
Castle Place, 166 High Street, Lewes, East Sussex, England BN7 1XU
Distributed in Australia by Capricorn Link (Australia) Pty. Ltd.
P.O. Box 704, Windsor, NSW 2756, Australia

I'm Going To Read is a trademark of Sterling Publishing Co., Inc.

Library of Congress Cataloging-in-Publication Data

Ziefert, Harriet.
   Tic and Tac / Harriet Ziefert ; pictures by Elliot Kreloff.
      p. cm.—(I'm going to read)
   Summary: Two cats, Tic and Tac, play hide-and-seek in a tree.
   ISBN-13: 978-1-4027-3432-8
   ISBN-10: 1-4027-3432-8
   [1. Cats—Fiction. 2. Hide-and-seek—Fiction.] I. Kreloff, Elliot, ill.
   II. Title. III. Series.
   PZ7.Z487Thu 2006
   [E]—dc22   2005034432

Printed in China
All rights reserved

Sterling ISBN-13: 978-1-4027-3432-8
ISBN-10: 1-4027-3432-8

For information about custom editions, special sales, premium and
corporate purchases, please contact Sterling Special Sales
Department at 800-805-5489 or specialsales@sterlingpub.com.

TIC and TAC

Pictures by Elliot Kreloff

Sterling Publishing Co., Inc.
New York

are   hide-and-seek   cats

Chapter 1

Hide-and-Seek

Where are the cats?

is   tree   Tac   under

Tic is up . . .
up in a tree.

Tac is under . . .
under the tree.

Tac meows.

He wants Tic to come down.

Tic looks down at Tac.
Then she jumps higher!

Tic is still up in the tree.

Tac is still under the tree.

Tac meows.
He still wants Tic to come down.

climbs   see

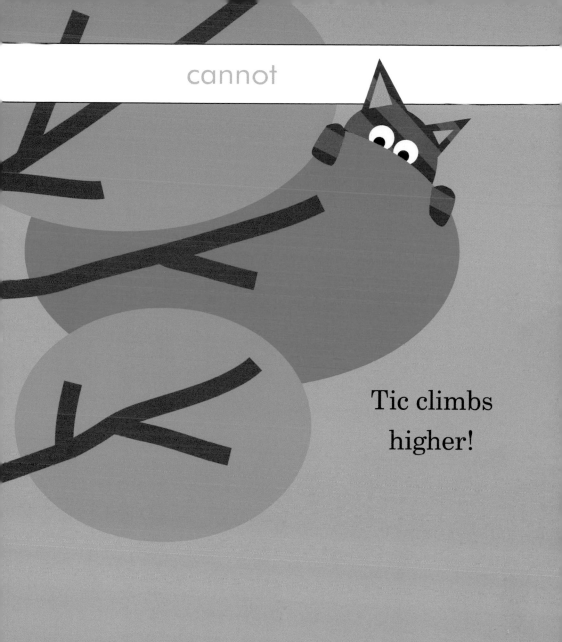

Tic climbs
higher!

Tac cannot see Tic.

Tic hides.

Tac seeks.

Where is Tic?
Where is she?

Where is Tac?
Where is he?

Two cats play hide-and-seek
in a tree.

Chapter 2

New Game

Two cats play a new game.

Tic runs.
Tac runs after her.

Tac chases Tic
around and around.

Tac runs.
Tic runs after him.

Tic chases Tac
around and around.

Rover comes.

He chases Tac and Tic.

Tic and Tac run to the tree.

Rover is under
the tree.

WOOF

Tic and Tac
are up in the tree.

Rover barks.
He wants Tic and Tac
to come down.

Tic looks at Tac.

Tac looks at Tic.

And then . . .

jump

they

Two cats and a dog play
a new game under a tree!